MW01502892

Zookeepers

Tony Hyland

Smart Apple Media

This edition first published in 2006 in the United States of America by Smart Apple Media.

Smart Apple Media
2140 Howard Drive West
North Mankato
Minnesota 56003

First published in 2005 by
MACMILLAN EDUCATION AUSTRALIA PTY LTD
627 Chapel Street, South Yarra, Australia 3141

Visit our website at www.macmillan.com.au

Associated companies and representatives throughout the world.

Library of Congress Cataloging-in-Publication Data

Hyland, Tony.
    Zookeepers / by Tony Hyland.
    p. cm. – (Extreme jobs)
    Includes index.
    Contents: Do you want to be a zoo keeper? – A zoo keeper's day – Risks and dangers – Training – Zoos in history – Zoo jobs. Gorilla keepers ; Raptor keepers ; Lion keepers ; Reptile and amphibian keepers ; Marine mammal keepers ; Aquarists ; Curators ; Zoo vets – Could you be a zoo keeper?
    ISBN-13: 978-1-58340-740-0
    1. Zoos–Vocational guidance–Juvenile literature. 2. Zoo keepers–Juvenile literature. I. Title.

    QL50.5.H95 2006
    636.088'9023–dc22   2005056799

Edited by Ruth Jelley
Text and cover design by Peter Shaw
Page layout by SPG
Photo research by Legend Images

Printed in USA

Acknowledgments
The author is grateful for the assistance provided by Zoos Victoria in providing background information and arranging interviews and photos for this book. The New England Aquarium, Shedd Aquarium, and Durrell Wildlife Conservation Trust also provided valuable assistance.
The author and the publisher are grateful to the following for permission to reproduce copyright material:

Cover photograph: Snow leopard, routine inspection at Taronga Zoo, Sydney, courtesy of Greg Wood/AFP/ Getty Images

Durrell Wildlife Conservation Trust, p. 13 top; Tom Davies, Durrell Wildlife Conservation Trust, p. 15; PORNCHAI KITTIWONGSAKUL/AFP/Getty Images, p. 8; Harry Todd/Fox Photos/Getty Images, p. 12; Greg Wood/AFP/Getty Images, pp. 1, 4; Josephine Hyland, pp. 7, 10, 14 bottom, 16, 17, 21, 28, 29; © John G. Shedd Aquarium, pp. 23, 23; Brett Dennis/Lochman Transparencies, p. 6; Gerald Kuchling/Lochman Transparencies, p. 27; Dennis Sarson/Lochman Transparencies, p. 5; Melbourne Aquarium, p. 24; Melbourne Zoo, p. 14 top; Photodisc, p. 30; Sarah Saunders, pp. 9, 11, 13 bottom, 18, 19, 20, 22, 26; Heather Urquhart, p. 25 (both).

Contents

Glossary words
When a word is printed in **bold**, you can look up its meaning in the Glossary on page 31.

Do you want to be a zookeeper?

Zoo vets look after a wide range of animals.

The lions are roaring for their food, the monkey cage needs cleaning, and there's a baby wombat that must be bottle-fed.

This is the world of zookeepers—busy, possibly dangerous, but never dull. Some zookeepers only look after one type of animal. Others work with everything from elephants to chimpanzees. Zoo vets see more unusual animals in a week than most vets would see in a lifetime.

A zookeeper's job is always an adventure. It really is an extreme job. Zookeepers work with animals of all types; large and fierce, cute and cuddly, and everything in between. The work is sometimes hard, and can be dangerous. But it is also an adventure. Most zookeepers think they have the best job in the world.

Perhaps you could be a zookeeper one day.

What is a zoo?

Zoos are places where wild animals are kept. Some are small zoos with a few animals. Others are huge open areas, where the animals roam free. Even fish and other sea creatures are kept in zoos.

At small zoos there is little room for the animals to move about. The animals live in small **enclosures**, where the public can come up close to watch them. **Open-range zoos** are as big as farms. They have large open areas where animals such as zebras and rhinoceroses can roam around freely. Visitors are usually guided through on buses.

Aquariums are zoos for fish and other sea creatures. The enclosures have glass walls so that people can see the creatures in their natural environment. **Oceanariums** usually keep larger sea mammals, such as seals, dolphins, and even whales.

Every year, millions of visitors come to see animals, such as this orangutan, in zoos all over the world.

A zookeeper's day

Zookeepers are busy all day. Their main job is caring for the animals. Most zookeepers work with a small group of animals. Some will work with the big cats, while others may work with **birds of prey**.

EXTREME INFO

How do you catch a tiger?

When the vet needs to examine a tiger, zookeepers fire a dart containing **anesthetic**. While the tiger is unconscious, the vet and keepers can check it, and operate on it if necessary.

Zookeepers prepare healthy, nutritious food for their animals. They use only the freshest fruits and vegetables. They also clean cages and enclosures daily. Zookeepers watch the animals while they are feeding them and cleaning out their enclosures. Zookeepers must make sure that the animals look healthy and are eating well. If there is a problem with one of the animals, they call in the zoo vet.

Zookeepers must also be friendly and helpful to people who visit the zoo. People often ask questions about the animals.

Zookeepers keep at a safe distance when handling dangerous animals, such as crocodiles.

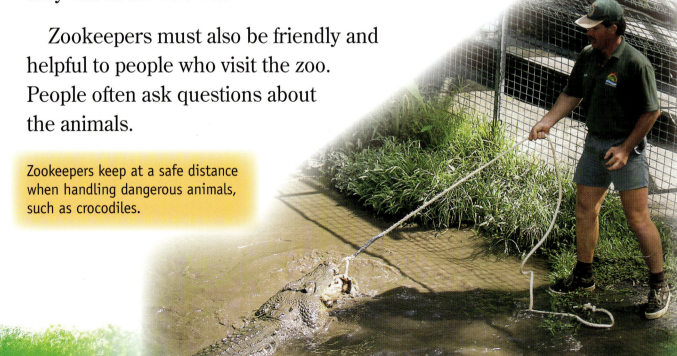

Training animals

Zookeepers usually train the zoo animals. They spend time getting the animals used to having contact with humans. Zoo animals need to accept their keepers, and not run away as animals would in the wild. Zookeepers use small food treats to reward them. Day by day, they persuade the animal to come a little closer. Eventually, the zookeepers can train them to do things such as moving out of an enclosure at cleaning time.

Training the animals in this way is called conditioning. It makes life easier for both the keepers and the animals. When the keepers need to clean the enclosure or treat a minor injury, the animals don't run away in panic.

This tree kangaroo, Timmy, takes a snack from the zookeeper's hands.

EXTREME INFO

Enriching environment

Zookeepers try to make life more interesting for their animals. They give the animals unusual things to see or smell. Sometimes they hide food, so that the animals have to search for it.

Risks and dangers

Zookeepers deal with risks and dangers every day. They are trained to deal safely with wild animals. However, it can still be dangerous. Some of the risks for zookeepers are:

Animal attack	Large meat-eaters such as lions can inflict terrible injuries with their teeth and claws. Rhinoceroses, hippopotamuses, and elephants can be dangerous. Even a bad-tempered monkey can give a nasty bite.
Disease	Some diseases pass from animals to humans. Zoo animals live in healthy conditions, but diseases such as **bird flu** can be brought in by wild birds.
Escaped animals	Escaped animals become lost and frightened. They can lash out at keepers trying to recapture them.
Accidental injuries	Accidents can happen, even to careful workers. Animals that are large or have sharp teeth, beaks, or claws can injure keepers without meaning to. Zoo work is often hard and physical. Keepers work outside in all weather conditions.

Zookeepers are trained to handle dangerous animals, such as crocodiles, safely.

Zoo security

One of the first things new zookeepers learn about is security. This means keeping the animals safely locked up at all times. Zoo enclosures are always kept locked. Escaped animals can be a threat to the public, and to their own safety. Even if the animal is not dangerous to people, it can hurt itself.

Keepers unlock and re-lock gates dozens of times every single day. Each enclosure has two gates. The keeper unlocks the first gate, goes in and re-locks it, then unlocks the second gate. The animals have no chance to escape. For dangerous animals, there is a red warning tag on the lock.

Zookeepers unlock gates many times each day.

EXTREME INFO

Emergency signals

Zookeepers wear a two-way radio at all times. If there is an emergency, they can call for help. If the keeper is knocked down, the radio automatically sends out an emergency signal.

Check all slide locked before

Training

Modern zookeepers often train in **zoology** or **biology** at college. Students who do these courses study animals, learning how their bodies work and how they live in the wild.

Students sometimes volunteer to work at a zoo during school holidays. When the zoo needs a new keeper, the staff might be glad to hire an eager young volunteer. Other trainee zookeepers do a zookeeper course like an **apprenticeship.** They work at the zoo most days and study part-time at a technical college.

Experienced zookeepers never stop learning. They can train to become senior keepers, or become specialists in their favorite animal.

EXTREME INFO

Step by step

The main steps for a career as a zookeeper are:

- Zookeeper
- Head keeper
- Curator or Senior keeper
- Director

Kellie Watson loves her job as a bird keeper.

Working with other zoos

Zoos around the world work together to help each other. The easiest way to help is to swap information about animal care. If zookeepers have a problem with an animal, they can ask other zoos for help. There are no secrets between zoos. Zookeepers are happy to help each other.

Zoos often exchange animals. If they have too many of one kind, they will send some to another zoo. Zoos do not buy or sell these animals. They simply do what is best for the animals. Zoos also exchange people. Keepers sometimes go to live in another country, to see how zoos work in other parts of the world. This helps the keepers to understand their animals better. It also means that most zookeepers have friends at many other zoos. When they need advice from an overseas zoo, they can usually contact someone they know there.

This zookeeper exchanges e-mails with other keepers around the world.

11

Zoos in history

Animals in the early zoos lived in small, cramped cages.

There were no real zoos in ancient days. Traders sometimes brought strange animals, such as lions or elephants, from far away.

Animals like this were not treated well. They were often locked in tiny cages. Curious people would come to tease and torment the animals. The Romans of 2,000 years ago held wild animal fights for the public. The animals were made to fight each other, or to fight humans.

The first real zoos were built in the 1800s. They were called menageries. Again, animals were kept in cramped cages with concrete floors and steel bars. Zookeeper jobs were not popular. The zookeepers knew very little about how to look after the animals. Many animals died because they were poorly cared for. In many menageries, animals were trained to do silly tricks. Chimpanzees were often dressed up and put on display for people to laugh at.

Changing the zoos

People who had seen animals running free in the wild wanted to change the way zoos worked. They designed larger and more comfortable enclosures for the animals. Zookeepers began to feed their animals the food they would find in their natural **habitat**.

Today, zookeepers design enclosures that look like natural habitats. Pandas live in bamboo forests. Gorillas roam around in enclosures that look like rain forests. Giraffes and zebras mix with rhinoceroses in huge open fields that look like the plains of Africa. Modern zoos are far different to the old menageries. The animals are well cared for by people who are experts in animal care.

Giraffes and zebras roam free in this modern zoo.

Zoo jobs

Gorilla keepers

Gorillas are the largest of the apes. Their natural habitat is the rain forest of Africa, but they are an endangered species.

Gorilla keepers don't normally go into the gorilla enclosure. Gorillas are so strong that even friendly contact could injure a human. Modern gorilla enclosures have plenty of rocks, trees, bushes, and caves. Gorillas eat large quantities of fresh fruit and vegetables every day, along with leaves and stems of plants. Preparing this food is a major task for the keepers.

Each day when the gorillas are locked away, keepers hide things in unusual places in the enclosure. Searching for interesting things, such as food treats, keeps the gorillas occupied.

Baby gorillas

Gorilla mothers in zoos often don't look after their babies well. Zookeepers help to care for the babies, looking after them in a gorilla nursery. Baby gorillas rejoin their mothers when they are older.

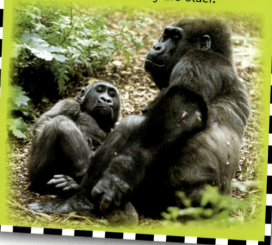

Preparing food for the gorillas takes a lot of time.

Conservation of gorillas in the wild

Gorillas in the wild are endangered. One threat to gorillas is poaching, or illegal hunting. Poachers hunt the gorillas for meat and for trophies. Gorillas are also threatened by rain forest clearing.

Gorilla keepers work to save this species. They breed large numbers of gorillas in captivity. However, these gorillas can't be sent to Africa, because they would die there. Many zoos help by sending keepers to Africa where they can work with the local people. The keepers teach the people to care for the gorillas, and to restore their habitat.

RISK FACTOR

Gorilla keepers have a rewarding job, but they deal with risks, such as:

- unlocked cages
- attack by a frightened gorilla
- being injured by an overly friendly gorilla

A gorilla expert works with African people to protect the local gorillas.

Zoo jobs

Raptor keepers

Raptors are fierce birds of prey.
They include eagles, hawks, falcons, and owls.
Raptors have curved, sharp beaks and powerful **talons**.
Zookeepers train these birds using techniques that
have been used for hundreds of years.

Hunters have trained hawks and falcons for over 3,000 years. Zookeepers use the same training techniques that hunters have used for hundreds of years. In some zoos, raptors are trained to put on displays for the public. Audiences are amazed as eagles and falcons swoop overhead and then settle on the keeper's arm.

Raptors work best if they can bond with just one or two keepers. Raptor keepers often work with the same birds for many years. They train their birds, using small pieces of food as a reward.

A raptor keeper shows a nankeen kestrel to the crowd.

Richard Naisbitt

Richard Naisbitt learned to train falcons when he lived in Africa.

Raptor keeper

Job

I'm the keeper in charge of raptors at Healesville Sanctuary near Melbourne, Australia.

Experience

I started training falcons when I was nine years old in Zimbabwe. Later, I became a safari guide and wildlife officer. I've spent thousands of hours in the field, releasing and tracking raptors. I've also written a book about treating captive raptors.

My work

I put on daily shows with birds of prey. I also help to **rehabilitate** injured wild birds brought in by the public.

My scariest moment

In Zimbabwe, I set a peregrine falcon off to fly, and saw it come down in thick scrub. When I went in after it I walked into a lion. Fortunately, the lion roared and ran off.

Things I don't like

I don't like being bitten and scratched by the raptors. Raptors can do serious damage which can hurt, but that's part of the job.

Richard Naisbitt's favourite eagle is Jess.

Zoo jobs

Lion keepers

Lion keepers care for the largest of the big cats. Most wild lions live on the plains of Africa where they hunt zebra and wildebeest. Zoo lions cannot live by hunting.

Lion keepers have a busy job. They start early, preparing the enclosure for the day. The keepers provide something unusual each day to make the lions' day more interesting. It could be bunches of strong-smelling herbs, or manure from the zebra enclosure. The lions find zebra manure fascinating and rather puzzling. Wild lions track the scent of a herd of zebra and their manure when they are hunting. Zoo lions will never get the chance to hunt zebra like they would in the wild.

Once the lions are let out for the day, the keeper starts preparing their food. Each lion gets about 9 pounds (4 kg) of meat a day.

A lion keeper sprinkles herbs throughout the enclosure to give the lions something interesting to smell.

Making the lion enclosure safe

Modern lion enclosures are grassy and open. They look like the grassy African plains. They are usually surrounded by a wide, deep **moat**, and a tall steel fence. The lions are released into the public enclosure during the day. The lions know it is time to return to their cages late in the day. Like most other zoo animals, they have been trained to do this by their keepers, using food rewards.

Lion keepers take extra precautions with locks and cages. The doors are remotely controlled. No one wants to let lions loose.

A strong steel fence keeps the lions safely in their enclosure.

RISK FACTOR

Lion keepers take extra care. They try to prevent risks, such as:

- lions escaping from unlocked cages
- entering a lion cage by mistake
- being injured by an escaped lion

19

Zoo jobs

Reptile and amphibian keepers

Keeping reptiles and amphibians is one of the more difficult zoo jobs. Snakes, lizards, crocodiles, and turtles are all reptiles. Frogs are amphibians.

Reptiles and frogs need more care than most other zoo creatures. Their enclosures must be kept at the right temperature at all times to prevent illness. Desert creatures are kept in a dry, sandy enclosure. Rain forest creatures are kept in a warm, moist enclosure. During cold weather, most reptiles and frogs **hibernate**. Zookeepers trick the creatures into staying alert by keeping their enclosures at a steady temperature throughout the year.

Some reptiles move very quickly. Their keepers must be careful when opening enclosures or the creatures could escape.

EXTREME INFO

What's for lunch?

Most snakes only eat about once a week. Zookeepers feed them dead mice or day-old chicks. The animals are killed humanely, because it is against zoo policy to use live creatures as food.

A reptile keeper checks the turtles in their heated enclosure.

Conserving reptiles in the wild.

Zookeepers play a part in conserving reptiles and amphibians in the wild. In many parts of the world, reptiles are endangered. When people drain swamps and clear forests they destroy the reptiles' habitat. People often do not care what happens to reptiles because they are not cute and cuddly. When a new airport was built in Hong Kong, zookeepers helped to save the native frogs, whose habitat was destroyed.

In Vietnam, a local freshwater turtle is endangered. Chris Banks, a reptile curator working in Australia, travels to Vietnam to help save these endangered turtles. He helps the Saigon Zoo staff to educate the public, using posters and children's books. Reptile keepers in zoos everywhere try to show visitors that even poisonous snakes deserve protection.

RISK FACTOR

Reptile keepers take special care with their creatures. They face risks such as:

- reptiles escaping
- bites and scratches
- poisonous snake bites

Chris Banks has helped to save endangered turtles in Asia.

Zoo jobs

Marine mammal keepers

Dolphins, whales, and seals are kept in oceanariums. These marine mammals are lively and intelligent.

Marine mammal specialists are often performers as well as keepers. Every day, they pull on their wetsuits and run their animals through spectacular tricks. Marine mammal keepers work as hard as other zookeepers. They feed their animals, watch their health closely, and keep the enclosures clean.

Marine mammal keepers develop a close relationship with the animals in their care. The "tricks" the animals perform are really natural behavior that they would do in the wild. Keepers train the animals to perform by using small rewards, such as food.

EXTREME INFO

How big is a killer whale?

Orcas, or killer whales, are the world's largest dolphins. Male orcas grow to between 20 and 26 feet (6–8 m) long, and weigh between 7,900 and 11,900 pounds (3,600–5,400 kg). Female orcas are slightly shorter and lighter, growing up to about 7,900 pounds (3,600 kg).

Some dolphin keepers let visitors come close to their dolphins.

Ken Ramirez

Marine mammal trainer

Ken Ramirez trains whales and other sea mammals.

Job

I'm in charge of the animal care and training programs at Shedd Aquarium in Chicago.

Experience

I trained guide dogs while I was in high school. At college I volunteered to work at a **marine park**, helping with dolphin and killer whale shows. Since then, I've worked with dolphins, whales, sea lions, seals, and otters.

Why I do this job

My love of animals got me into this field. I'm proud of the good work that we can do through training our animals. We improve the quality of their lives and share our knowledge with our visitors.

Physical challenges

Working with animals requires physical strength and fitness. As I get older, the challenges of diving in cold water, lifting heavy objects, and working long hours get harder.

Most exciting experience

Getting in the water with a killer whale or any other animal, and developing a relationship with that animal.

Ken Ramirez plays with Naya, the beluga whale.

Zoo jobs

Aquarists

Aquarium keepers are called aquarists. Aquariums are zoos for fish and other sea creatures. Aquariums, with their huge glass windows, allow people to see what life is like under the sea.

Like other zookeepers, aquarists have a daily round of feeding the creatures and cleaning the enclosures. If the enclosures are not kept clean, the water becomes dirty and cloudy. This is bad for the fish and also for the public who come to watch.

It's difficult to keep fish in captivity. The water temperature, light, and food must be just right, or the fish become sick and die.

People who visit aquariums can see how fish live in the sea.

Heather Urquhart

Senior aquarist

Heather Urquhart is in charge of the penguins at the New England Aquarium.

Job

I work with the penguins at the New England Aquarium in Boston. We have three species: African, Rockhopper, and Little Blue or Fairy penguins.

Experience

I studied biology at college and volunteered to work at the Aquarium when I was a student.

My daily tasks

My main task is the care and feeding of our 64 penguins. Wearing a wetsuit, I feed the penguins in the exhibit twice a day. I also attend to the penguins' medical needs with the vets, and help to raise baby penguins.

My conservation work

I have worked in South Africa, Namibia, New Zealand, Australia, and Chile to help protect the native penguin populations.

Why I do this job

I wanted to work with animals and I loved the ocean. After viewing a Jacques Cousteau television program, I knew the animals of the marine world were my passion.

Heather feeds the penguins.

Zoo jobs

Curators

E_XTREME INFO

Saving a war-torn zoo

The zoo at Kabul, in Afghanistan, was badly damaged by many years of war and fighting. Senior zoo curators from all over the world raised money and donated animals to help the zoo rebuild its enclosures and start a fresh collection of animals.

Curators, or senior zookeepers, are the most experienced keepers at the zoo.

Curators are zookeepers who have spent years learning how to deal with the animals in their care. When the other keepers have a problem with an animal, the curator will probably know the solution. If not, the curator can contact other senior zookeepers around the world.

Senior zookeepers organize the zoo. They are in charge of the other keepers, and make sure that the animals are well cared for. Curators help to design new **exhibits** and enclosures. With careful planning, keepers can design enclosures that look like natural habitat for the animals, but still let visitors see the creatures easily.

A senior zookeeper checks that the tree kangaroo is well cared for.

How senior zookeepers can help

Senior zookeepers often travel to other countries. They work with zoos in other parts of the world, to improve care for their animals. They also often help to conserve endangered creatures. They can work with local people to get changes made to **conservation laws**.

When a small island near Mauritius was taken over by rabbits and goats, the rare wild animals of the island were almost wiped out. Gerald Durrell and other senior keepers from the Jersey Zoo flew out to help save animals such as the Round Island gecko. They organized local people to remove the rabbits and goats. Soon the native animals and plants began to **regenerate**. The gecko and other creatures are now safe on their island home.

RISK FACTOR

Curators work with animals every day. They face risks, such as:

- bites and scratches
- escaping animals
- disease passed on from animals

The Round Island Gecko is one of many animals saved by senior zookeepers from Jersey Zoo.

Zoo jobs

Zoo vets

Most vets just see dogs and cats. Zoo vets deal with every type of creature, from a tiny frog to a huge rhinoceros.

It takes many years of study to become a zoo vet. First, they train to be a normal veterinarian. Then they do three or more years of specialist zoo training. Most zoo vets do this training in the U.K. or U.S.

Every day, the vet hears reports from the keepers of any sick animals. Sometimes the problems are small. At other times, the vet must perform a major operation. Vets deal with many unusual problems, from elephants with sore feet to baby meerkats that won't eat.

Zoo vet, Geoff Pye, checks a baby meerkat.

A job for the zoo vet

Every day, zoo vets do jobs that no other vet would do. Zoo vet, Geoff Pye, had to treat a white rhinoceros calf that was suffering from **hypothermia**. He wanted to move the baby to a sheltered area, but the mother rhinoceros would not let him come near. Zookeepers in trucks helped to separate the baby from its mother. Geoff loaded the baby rhinoceros onto one of the trucks, and the other trucks drove away. The mother rhinoceros angrily chased the trucks, but they wove from side to side, confusing her.

Geoff placed the baby in a sheltered spot before the mother caught up. The mother and baby were only separated for about 20 minutes. They stayed in the sheltered area, and soon the baby fed again.

Geoff Pye and the white rhinoceroses he treated.

RISK FACTOR

Zoo vets see every type of animal. They are careful of risks, such as:

- accidental injury from the animals
- bites and scratches.

Could you be a zookeeper?

You could be a zookeeper if you:

- have normal health
- are reasonably fit
- enjoy working with animals
- are calm and patient
- enjoy being active outdoors
- are prepared to work hard
- are sensible and responsible

If you prefer to be a scientist, you could study biology or zoology, or become a zoo vet. You'll still spend a lot of time working with animals.

Do you love playing with your pets? Then you're well on the way to becoming a zookeeper!

If you love animals, you could become a zookeeper.

 Glossary

anesthetic	a chemical that makes an animal unconscious
apprenticeship	the period of being an apprentice, where a person learns a trade while working at it
biology	the branch of science for the study of living things
bird flu	an infectious disease of birds, which can be passed onto humans
birds of prey	hunting bird, such as eagle, hawk, or owl
conservation laws	laws designed to protect animals and the environment
enclosures	closed-in spaces for keeping zoo animals
endangered	in danger of extinction
exhibits	displays
habitat	natural home of any creature
hibernate	sleep through the winter
hypothermia	having a dangerously low body temperature
marine park	zoo for displaying marine animals such as dolphins and whales
moat	deep ditch around an enclosure, sometimes filled with water
oceanariums	zoos for displaying marine animals such as dolphins and whales
open-range zoos	zoos where animals are kept in large open areas, rather than cages
regenerate	to grow back again
rehabilitate	to return animals to their wild state
talons	claws, especially on birds of prey
zoology	the branch of science for the study of animal life

Index

7-01